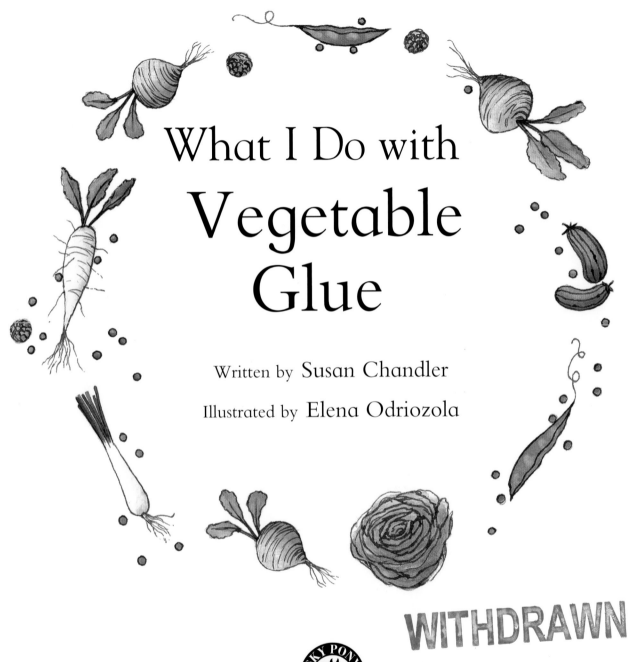

What I Do with Vegetable Glue

Written by Susan Chandler

Illustrated by Elena Odriozola

Sky Pony Press
New York

When my right arm fell off,
I knew what to do,

I stuck it back on,
With vegetable glue.

When my head rolled away,
I thought it had gone,

But I found it again,
And stuck it back on.

You can see for yourself,
That something's not right,
People don't fall apart.
It's just not polite.

I have to keep with me,
A big tub of glue,
To stick parts back on,
To make good as new.

Vegetable
Glue

I hear you all shout,
"We've heard quite enough!
Tell us, how do we make,
That gloopy green stuff?"

"If our noses fall off,
Then what would we do?
Where would we buy
Some vegetable glue?"

Well, it's not in the stores,
And it's not on the telly,
Because vegetable glue
Is in everyone's belly.

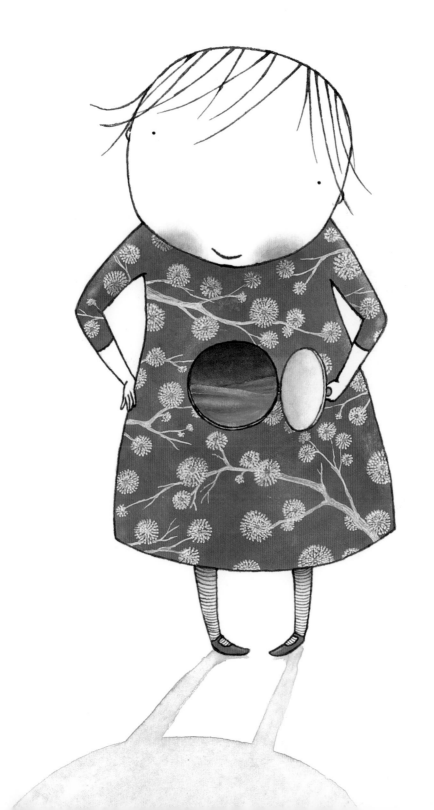

When you eat up your greens
Your body makes glue,
Which keeps all your parts
Still sticking to you.

But I was quite silly,
I made a mistake.
I wouldn't eat good things,
I only ate…

...cake!

I wouldn't eat cabbage,
Or turnips or beans,
I didn't like carrots,
I didn't like greens.

I didn't eat sprouts,
Now I've no special glue
No goodness inside me,
Like other kids do.

While others are playing,
I can't even cough.
If I sneeze or I burp,
Then something falls off.

Oops, pardon me
I've made a rude sound.
My bottom's dropped off

And is now…

…on the ground.

Now here is my granny
To give me some more.
She's looking quite good
For a hundred and four.

She'd like you to know
Why she's so fit and able.
She ate all her greens
Before leaving the table.

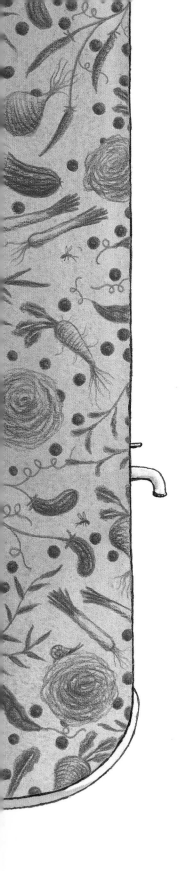

She ate all her greens
And I hope you do too,

Then...

you'll never need...

...any vegetable glue.

For Chris and Ted

S. C.

For My Mothers

E. O.

Library of Congress Cataloging-in-Publication Data

Chandler, Susan, 1971-
[Vegetable glue]
What I do with vegetable glue / Susan Chandler ; illustrated by Elena Odriozola.
p. cm.
Summary: Illustrations and rhyming text introduce a little girl who only eats cake and, lacking "good stuff" inside to keep her body together, must use her grandmother's vegetable glue to reattach parts that fall off.
ISBN 978-1-61608-661-9 (hardcover : alk. paper)
[1. Stories in rhyme. 2. Food habits--Fiction. 3. Nutrition--Fiction.] I. Odriozola, Elena, ill. II. Title.
PZ8.3.C362Wh 2012
[E]--dc23
2011047205